Sandy Goes to Dog School

SANDY
Goes To Dog School

AUTHOR J.D. THOMAS
ILLUSTRATED BY LESLIE SPRADLIN

Xulon Press
2301 Lucien Way #415
Maitland, FL 32751
407.339.4217
www.xulonpress.com

Printed in the United States of America.

Paperback ISBN-13: 978-1-6312-9806-6

Ebook ISBN-13: 978-1-6312-9807-3

Sandy Gets into Trouble

"Mom, Sandy is eating my cereal!" John shouted. "Sandy, stop that and get down from there" John's mother said. When Sandy heard John's mother say stop, Sandy jumped off the chair. When Sandy jumped she knocked over the cereal dish and fruit bowl. Milk, cereal, apples, and bananas flew into the air and onto the table, chair, and floor! What a mess it was!

The children's father said, "This is the second time Sandy has been
eating off our kitchen table, what kind of behavior is this? Sandy
will have to go to dog school to learn how to behave in our home.
When Sandy heard the children's father say this she walked away sad,
because she knew she did something wrong.

Miss Fussykins School for Dogs

The children asked, "What will Sandy learn at dog school?" "The dog school will teach Sandy to sit, shake hands, eat from her own dish, and not our table," said their father. "We will go with Sandy and watch her as she learns," said their mother.

Many people brought their dogs to Miss Fussykins school so their dogs would learn how to behave.

"Good morning everyone, my name is Miss Fussykins, I am going to teach each dog in this class how to behave correctly and properly," said Miss Fussykins."When our class is finished, each dog will receive their own special diploma. A diploma is a paper that says your dog has completed our class, and will behave themselves when they go home."

The Dogs First Lesson

"Good morning class, today I am going to teach your dogs to sit and shake hands," said Miss Fussykins. She walked over to Sandy and picked up her paw with her hand. Miss Fussykins said, "Now everyone watch as I teach Sandy to shake hands. Sandy, shake!" but Sandy just looked at her and laid down.

"No, No, you are doing it all wrong. Now let's try this again. Sandy sit, good dog, now Sandy shake!" but Sandy did not shake her hand, she laid down and rolled over!

"No, no, no, you're doing it all wrong! If you want to graduate dog school you have to do what I tell you. Now lets try this one more time. Sandy, sit! Now Sandy, shake hands!" but Sandy just looked at Miss Fussykins and barked: "Ruff, Ruff, Ruff."

Sandy and the Doughnut

When Sandy walked past the snack table at dog school, she bumped into a tray of doughnuts. One doughnut fell onto Sandy's head! "What is going on here? Now Sandy is taking doughnuts from the snack table? Sandy come here and give me that doughnut!" said Miss Fussykins. Sandy walked over to her and Miss Fusssykins took the doughnut off her head and threw it in the garbage can. When the people in the room saw this they started laughing.

Sandy Wears a Jacket

Everyone hung their jackets on the hooks that were against the wall. As Sandy walked past the jackets, one jacket slipped off the hook and onto Sandy's back.

Miss Fussykins was telling everyone that it is important not to let their dogs chew on shoes. She said they should give their dogs a chew toy to bite on. As she was talking, Sandy walked right in front of her with a red jacket on her back! When Miss Fussykins saw this she became very upset. "I can't believe this, now she is wearing some-ones jacket! Whoever heard of such poor behavior as this. Sandy is not going to graduate this class and get her diploma if she keeps misbehaving." One of the children said, "You can't blame Sandy, she is just a puppy." Miss Fussykins said, "You may be right, but if Sandy gets into anymore trouble, I will not be happy".

Do you think Sandy will get into more trouble?

Sandy Helps the Teacher

The next day, when the parents and children brought their dogs
Miss Fussykins school for dogs, Miss Fussykins said, "I'm sorry to te
you all there will be no school today. We can't get into the scho
because I lost my keys. I will have to go home and look for them." A
everyone started to leave, one child said, " Look! That dog has four
your keys! Sandy found your keys."

When Miss Fussykins saw this she said, "Sandy thank you so much for finding my keys. Here is a delicious healthy snack for you." She gave Sandy some frozen string beans to eat.

The Graduation Party

Miss Fussykins said, "Tomorrow is the big graduation day. Each dog that has learned how to behave properly will get a special graduation hat, and a Doggy Diploma!" The next day everyone arrived at the dog school with their dogs.

Just before the graduation party was about to begin, Sandy walked past the jackets hanging on the wall. Can you guess what happened? Yes, a jacket fell onto Sandy's back again! One girl said, "That dog is wearing my jacket!" Everyone was laughing, even Miss Fussykins thought Sandy looked funny.

Miss Fussykins said, "Sandy you are a funny dog. I know you are a good dog because you are friendly and kind to everyone. You love all the children and they love you. Congratulations Sandy, you have completed our dog class and you will receive your diploma. Now we will have a graduation party for everyone. Congratulations everybody!" Sandy barked, "Ruff, Ruff, Ruff, Arf, Arf, Arf!"

The Dogs Receive
Their Diplomas

Miss Fussykins called each dogs' name, and, one at a time, handed them their Doggy Diplomas. When she called Sandy's name, Sandy walked up to Miss Fussykins and shook her hand with her paw! Everyone clapped their hands.

UPS!

Then, they all sang a song that sounded like Happy Birthday to you, but their song had different words:

Happy Graduation to you,
Happy Graduation to you,
Happy Graduation dear doggies,
Happy graduation to you!

Sandy tried to sing too!

"Arf Arf Arf Arf Arf Arf Arf Arf!
Arf Arf Arf Arf Arf Arf Arf Arf!"

Goodbye Sandy!
We love you! See you next time.

CPSIA information can be obtained
at www.ICGtesting.com
Printed in the USA
BVHW020439170422
634266BV00002B/7